The Unrequited

By Niall Williams

NOVELS

Four Letters of Love
As it is in Heaven
The Fall of Light
Only Say the Word

PLAYS

A Little Like Paradise
The Way You Look Tonight

Niall Williams

The Unrequited

PICADOR SHOTS

First published 2006 by Picador
an imprint of Pan Macmillan Ltd
Pan Macmillan, 20 New Wharf Road, London N1 9RR
Basingstoke and Oxford
Associated companies throughout the world
www.panmacmillan.com

ISBN-13: 978-0-330-44583-2
ISBN-10: 0-330-44583-9

1 3 5 7 9 8 6 4 2

A CIP catalogue record for this book is available from
the British Library.

Typeset by Intype Libra Ltd
Printed and bound in Great Britain by
Mackays of Chatham plc, Chatham, Kent

HE WOKE IN THE sky, descending.

In the first moments of return he forgot
where he was and startled to see the pale floor
of cloud below. He was not himself. His head
propped to one side and his neck aching, briefly
he watched the sky as though it was a screen
awaiting a film. The density of cloud, the sense
of it being packed and firm, was unsettling.

Across his chest his arms were folded like
wings, rested or redundant. It was cold. In low
light about him others, sleeping with mouths
agape, appeared posed as in a tableau, a shut-eyed

sky-choir singing on mute as they plunged through cloud.

There had been an apology for the extreme coolness of the air, but he had missed it. He fingered the ache in his neck, astonished at the chill. In the dim light the backs of his hands were rivered a pale blue.

From behind a hostess arrived. A tall woman with blonde hair curled on top of her head, she wore the unreal expression an amateur draws on a first portrait. Her eyebrows were pencilled, her eyes green things you could not imagine capable of sight and there was not a single crease in the skin of her face.

'Sir?'

'Aren't we nearly there?'

'Very soon now, sir. Blanket?'

'No, thank you. I think I'll just get the heart pumping.'

In the hostess's eyes there was the mildest incomprehension.

'The heart. Blood. I'll walk up and down, I think.'

'You don't wish the blanket?'

'No. Thank you.'

'We will have fasten seatbelts soon.' Coolly she viewed him, then walked away.

Raphael Newell stretched his arms before him. It was, he thought, as though he had dreamt himself frozen. The dream had been so well done that he felt like an iceman. The plane steadying, the seatbelt sign still off, he stood at the head of the long cabin and looked down toward the rear. The seats were mostly empty. The passengers – businessmen and women, some tourists – preferred to sit singly in their own rows, or one took the aisle seat and the other the window, like pieces at the start of a game. As Ray moved through them toward the far galley, he paid little attention. He concentrated on the aches in his ankles and in not stumbling, but later he would recall a grey-suited Japanese dreaming with hands clasped between his knees, a pretty raven-haired woman in beige turtleneck, lipsticked mouth open as if for a kiss. There was a bald man in his late sixties with big black-framed glasses scowling in sleep, and mumbling something in German or Dutch that was per-haps a woman's name.

At the end of the aisle a bearded young man in a black wool jumper and hiking boots was blowing into his hands. He appeared prepared to arrive in the middle of rough terrain. To Ray he made what he must have considered the International Sign for Cold, arms crossed and his hands making a small slow up-and-down flapping.

'Very cold,' said Ray, stupidly.

The air was so intensely air-conditioned their breaths appeared before them.

'Ya.'

Ray tramped his feet and turned his head over one shoulder and then back over the other, stretching as it instructs in the Safety Guidelines for International Travellers.

'Any colder we die here,' said the hiker, 'plane of dead people arrive.' He blew in his hands, and stooped down to look out the window, which still revealed only cloud below. 'First time for you in Norway?'

'Yes.'

'You are a skier?'

'No, I'm not. Actually I'm just . . . visiting,' Ray said, because you don't tell another man you are flying to Oslo for love.

But above the dark beard the hiker's eyes glittered. 'Me too,' he said. 'Her name is Olga.'

There was no time for Ray's surprise. The seatbelt light came on and the hostess came sweeping down the aisle toward them, disapprovingly, as though they were pieces of litter previously attended to but somehow fallen onto the ground again.

'You must return, sirs,' she said sternly.

'Just stretching. Get the blood going, it's very cold.'

'You must return and sit down. We are there.'

'There? Are we? I didn't hear the announcement.'

With a series of flickerings, the lights came on and heads stirred. Returned to his seat, Ray watched compulsively the descent through cloud. It seemed a dense damp cloth, a thick substantial hemming between heaven and earth, not at all the thin wispy thing sentimentalists imagined. Minute after minute passed and still there was no end to it. It was blind and grey and relentless, and it occurred to Raphael Newell then what it would be like to be trapped within a cloud, to have no earth or sky appear, but always to be plunging desperately on in vain. The thought bloomed like black ink blotted. What if they were lost inside it? He touched his tongue to his lips; he held his hands. It was absurd. Of course they weren't, get a grip on yourself, Ray. Yet there was only the thick unforgiving cloud. Any moment now they would come out of it, and be returned to the world. Only they weren't. The descent and the cloud both endured. Ray turned from it and shut his eyes to think of the face of Helena Lund. But fear and falling robbed him of concentration.

Droplets of moisture appeared on the window travelling horizontally, the world falling sideways. What if *out* of the cloud at last there loomed a mountain? He wanted to cry out. Ray wanted to shout that things couldn't end like this, that he was living now for love, and had abandoned all else. He wanted to call out to God from the place He had hidden through all of Raphael Newell's life and say, not now, You cannot kill me now, You can't.

He wanted to shout, but he didn't. He stared out the window and moved both hands through his dark hair. He pulled the shirt collar wider.

It's like bloody gauze, he thought. There was a huge gauze curtain from floor to ceiling and he had run into it and from his thrashing to be free it had fallen on top of him, releasing spiders of fear. His panic found this image and made it vivid. Why were they not emerging from cloud? How deep could it be? He leaned toward the aisle to see if the hostess was alarmed. Strapped in her pull-down seat she stared ahead with perfect blankness. Other passengers too were anxious now. The whole plane had come alive.

Ray unsnapped his seatbelt to stand as though to shake off spiders, as though there might be air just above, for one insane moment thinking he might put his mouth against the air-vent and suck until the sky became blue.

'Sit down, sir. Sit down now!'

'I cannot breathe.'

'Sit. You must sit! We are there.'

'We are nowhere,' he said, 'look!' And as he

was pointing to the window the cloud like a curtain was pulled and suddenly revealed were vast dense forests of snow-powdered pine, and beyond them, in the approaching evening, the lights of Oslo.

2

How foolish he had been. He couldn't explain it to himself. He had flown twice before, and never experienced anything like it. Had the cloud been thicker than normal? Had their flight through it been longer? Perhaps it was just his desperation, his desire to arrive. International arrival does not allow for moments of personal pause, his bag was already on its way to the conveyor belt. He moved in the file of fellow passengers down the wheeled metal steps that adjoined the plane.

Raphael Newell was thirty-seven years of age.

An accountant at the small firm of Bradley & Whitton, Harcourt Street, Dublin, he was a mid-sized man with a quiet manner. The event of his life was loving his next-door neighbour Marjorie from the age of twelve until she discovered taller, better-looking men with danger in their eyes at age nineteen. She married one and disappeared into a life of disappointment in a stylish four-bedroomed house in the dull suburb of Greystones. But the fires of this devotion burned on in Raphael Newell for several years. He fuelled it with great chunks of broken heart and was not surprised when the few times he was pressed into going out with someone the relationship failed to spark. Softly the ashes built up inside him until at last Ray knew the love was extinguished when he could not find any more pieces of heart. He lived a small life. He focused on numbers. With a patient grey exactitude he balanced his clients' accounts and found on the margins of life a lesser contentment that was his.

After his parents' death, he bought a small house in Rathmines, and in the autumn, prompted by a radio ad, he enrolled himself in an evening class in 'art appreciation'. In early spring, as part of an organized tour, he visited Rome to see the ruins. After that, every year when the flier came in the post from the Dublin Centre for Adult Education, he read through it diligently and chose something for the winter. Perhaps because of his burdensome Christian name or because he still carried the urn of failed love, Raphael Newell was aware of not living up to something. He was conscious of a greater life, but mostly considered it was for others. Still, tentatively, he approached from the margins.

So, in some small measure to improve himself, he had attended a lecture at the Dublin Institute of Architecture on the theme of the religious imagination and its practical engagement with the realities of construction and engineering. He was not religious himself, but had the slow circumspection of an accountant who will not rule out anything completely until the final books have been done.

The evening of the lecture was lashed with rain. Dublin's trees had thrown down their leaves, and gutters pooled into the streets. Ray was glad of his umbrella. In the upstairs room in the old Georgian building red-velvet curtains were drawn. He sat on an aisle seat next to no one, furled and lay his umbrella underneath. He took out the small notepad he always carried and down-buttoned the top of his pen. The lecturer was from England and looked very brilliant, Ray thought, this would probably be very good. The audience was a scattered selection of students, religious, and those like himself enrolled for the autumn programme.

'What is the religious imagination? And how did it find form in the great churches of Europe? Was there such a thing as the concrete expression of divinity?' The lecturer floated the questions, and received a response of intelligent silence until the door opened and Helena Lund appeared. The room looked at her. A slim woman in her thirties with short fair hair, high, pronounced cheekbones and startling blue eyes, she wore a corona of raindrops.

'I'm very sorry,' she said, and pressed in past Raphael Newell's knees to sit beside him.

The lecturer resumed. He spoke quickly and moved back and forth on the narrow platform and had indeed the kind of cleverness often mistaken for brilliance. Images of the great churches appeared on slides overhead, and gave the audience the vertiginous impression of being a lower order of angels looking up at the spires from far below. It was during these moments of projection that under the guise of turning toward the screen in the centre Ray could look sidelong at the woman who smelled like almonds and rain.

He did not believe in love at first sight. He believed the force he was feeling was physical attraction, but it was so potent that he didn't want to look away. He wanted to stare at her. He had the profound sense of something familiar, but almost forgotten.

Helena Lund raised her hand.

'So you believe there will be no more churches?' Her accent had a faint colouring. The question allowed Ray to look at her.

'No more great ones,' the lecturer said, shuffling together his notes. 'In the twenty-first century I think we'll have difficulty achieving any sense of reality, never mind religion.' He slipped the notes inside his briefcase. 'Churches sprang from community. There are no communities now. Now a new catalogue of human experience exists, in which we become more and more separated from human reality, and each other, iPeople, the iGeneration. Maybe there'll be iChurches.'

There was a small laugh. He shrugged. The head of the Institute was standing by to thank him and ask for applause.

'What about love?' Helena Lund asked.

3

The Gardermoen airport, a high sweeping curve of glass and timber, was like ice architecture both firm and delicate. The evening sky roofed in blue light as the passengers headed to where their bags were already waiting, circling unclaimed on the conveyor belt with the kind of forlorn quality our objects have when separated from us. Ray waited for his case to come around. The cold of the plane was still with him, but his heart was racing furiously. It was an outrageous thing he was doing, flying to Oslo to find her, but as a consequence he already felt more alive than he had in years. He couldn't help smiling, and looked across the belt at the hiker and the raven-haired woman and the Japanese man and in his charged and almost beatific state it seemed to Ray they too were illumined with life, were each ready to run out into the world and love. The beauty of this childlike image turned his smile into a small irrepressible laugh. How good he felt! How sometimes everything could just shine!

Emboldened, believing in a triumphant love, he lifted his case and went to present his passport. The official took it without a word. Young, with a polished jaw and cheek structure that seemed to bestow superiority, he gave the passport serious scrutiny. Ray looked at the extraordinary ceiling, the great expanse of the blue. Impossible to imagine the thick cloud-cover now. When he looked back down, the official had his grey eyes turned on him.

'You?' he asked, and pointed to the photograph.

'Me? Of course, yes, me,' Ray said, and tapped the photograph and then his chest.

The official grimaced, as though Raphael Newell was a pain in his tooth, then he held up the open passport alongside the traveller's face.

'You are younger.'

'What? I'm sorry.'

'You are younger.'

'Was I? Well yes, it was, the photo was taken probably four or five years ago . . .'

'No. Now. Now you look younger than this.'

He placed the passport down on the desk, his hand holding it open. There was an instant of impasse. Then, whether from the awkwardness of having the man confess to cosmetic surgery, the growing impatience of travellers in the queue, or the sense this toothache could rage, the official lifted his stamp and thumped it down. 'Good for you,' he said.

Ray smiled. This was further proof that

what he felt was real; he was rejuvenated. He took back the passport and headed out through Nothing to Declare.

Night had fallen, the starry air sharp and startling. It was right, he thought, this is how Norway should be. The cold moved like a hand at the back of his neck. He pulled up his collars, stood in the taxi line, the plume of his breath coming and going. When his car came he was glad to slide into the warmth.

'I need a hotel,' he said, 'in the city centre. I have nothing booked.'

4

Helena Lund had come to Dublin to escape, she told him. It was after the lecture, she had apologized for being late, and Ray had told her there was no need. He pretended he hadn't even noticed. But he was glad nonetheless. He wouldn't have dared to speak to her otherwise. As he stepped out into the aisle he asked where she was from. He didn't look directly at her, he was afraid of her beauty.

'Oslo,' she said.

'Really?'

'You've been to Oslo?'

'No, no not at all. Just . . .' He looked at her. He couldn't help himself from looking at her. He looked the way you might look if somebody said, 'Here is the account of your future. Here is everything that's going to happen.' It was as if her face belonged in his life, though Ray couldn't explain that then.

'I escaped from Oslo.'

'Really?'

'O yes. Really. You are from Dublin?'

'Yes.' He was standing in the aisle, turned back to her, when she bent down and lifted his umbrella.

'Then you know someplace?' she asked. 'Where is the best hot chocolate in Dublin?'

When they arrived in the bar of the Gresham Hotel, Ray bought her the drink and asked her if he could ask her what she wanted to escape.

'My life, of course.' She lifted her left shoulder and dropped it as though checking a weight still there.

'I see,' he said. 'Was it something, something terrible that you needed to escape?'

'Nothing so terrible. Ordinary life, my husband, my children. Don't you want to escape your life? I escape, one week,' she said, 'and then I go back.'

Did he want to escape his life? It was a question that hadn't occurred to Ray until she asked it and by then he was already through its doorway. He was allowing himself to run into the space where he could look at her, where he could be standing beside this beautiful woman and feeling suddenly free as do those who are helplessly falling. There was the sheer thrill of it. There was a sense both strange and familiar, as if he knew her already, as if a life waits for just such a moment. Everything about her was illumined with revelation.

'Not for sex,' she said.

'Sorry?'

'Not for an affair. That's not why. I escape my life for life itself. You understand? You live with feeling of sadness, yes? Sadness because you are longing all the time, for something else,' she shrugged, 'for things to be otherwise sometimes *you want*. This is the condition of your living. You want many lives, not just this one. So, one week, I escape. I go and in this week try not to feel the sadness. I will see films, eat whatever, lie in a hot bath with music playing, go to galleries, go a lecture maybe, like this one tonight, I . . . whatever.'

'And then you will go back?'

'Then I go back.'

'Why? If it is sad there, why not stay here?'

She looked surprised by the question. Her lips pressed downward, her eyes narrowed. 'Sadness is not so easily escaped. Besides, I love my husband. I love my children,' she said.

Before she left that evening, Ray was emboldened to ask if he could see her again. He was still falling. He had already fallen past shyness and fear and discretion and the fuses in his eyes were flaring. She told him the following day she was going to Francis Bacon's reconstructed studio at the Hugh Lane Gallery.

'It is extraordinary, they say. To see what dirt was under his feet when he painted with his soul.'

He didn't know what to say to that. But then, before he had even considered, he said he would call in sick for work. He said he would meet her there at ten.

In Raphael Newell's dreams that night Helena Lund kept appearing. She appeared as herself, in white blouse and blue jeans; but each time he approached her, each time he reached out his hand, she became instead a moonlit church.

5

The Hotel Chester was where the taxi stopped. In a dark lobby of mahogany, marble and brass, Ray checked in. From the lounge behind reception a mournful piano music played. The pianist, an aged man in a black suit, raised his head to nod toward the new guest. In Room 111 Ray turned the heating up full. While the pipes clanked he stood by the window and looked at what he could see of Oslo. There was a grand avenue, slow steady traffic passing the grave facades of government buildings. In thick coats pallid-faced pedestrians moved briskly.

She was somewhere out there, he thought.

She was somewhere out there but she did not know yet that he had come. It was three weeks since he had seen her. He sat on the end of the bed, ran his right hand through his hair. He had no exact plan; he had only a compulsion, and a sense of never having lived before. Nothing was ever like this before. He was aware of an intensity in his perception, a sharpening, a brightening too, as if his spirit, his entire being, was *charged*. He sat on the bed and could not keep himself from smiling.

In the morning he would find her.

He went downstairs and from a pale young waitress with smoky eyes ordered a pork and potato stew. He had a fierce hunger; the food was hot and remarkably delicious and while he was eating there swept into the lounge a short moustachioed man in a black suit who came forward and extended his hand.

'Mr Newell, Mr Newell, welcome!' He wore his name on a small badge, Henrik Avner. 'You are very welcome.' He shook his guest's hand firmly. 'Everything is all right, the room?'

'Yes, yes. It's fine.'

'Good, very good. I am sorry I was not here to welcome you when you arrived. Anything you need, Mr Newell?'

'No, no thank you.'

Briefly Henrik Avner gazed at him, his two hands holding each other and his small eyes lit with some inner delight at this guest before him.

'Well, I leave you to your meal. It's good?'

'Very good, thank you.'

'Good, good. Welcome again, Mr Newell.'

He left as swiftly as he had arrived, leaving Raphael Newell bemused and inspired by the strangeness of such rapturous welcome. The stew was extraordinary but he was still hungry and ordered a second bowl of it. The aged pianist played a Chopin nocturne, the notes pealing with a sweet sadness. When the girl served the stew,

Raphael Newell thought she too seemed *pleased* with him. And, with the strange innocence of saints or lovers who see things with perfect simplicity, he came to think it was not because he was the only guest there, but rather that all saw upon him the mark of loving, as though it were a thing stamped on his forehead. When he rose the old man at the piano gave him another nod.

Outside, Ray walked in the cold to feel the reality of where he was and what he was doing. He went without a map and strode beneath the furred light of street lamps, turning up one street and down the next, noting names, Dronningen's Gate, Raadhusgata, Skippergata, and feeling an iron frost falling like bars across the stars. The skin of his face stung. The cold was startling and intense and he laughed out loud as he walked, thinking of the extremity as a pure and absolute condition in which the only unfreezing thing was his heart.

In the night city there were few cars and no

one walking. With silvered edge the ice air sliced free the top of his head and let his thoughts spill. I am here in Oslo. I have to see her. It doesn't matter what happens next.

6

He had arrived early at the Hugh Lane Gallery and stood beneath his black umbrella in the rain. He stood long enough to wonder if she was coming, long enough to feel foolish and for that to undress him of hope. It was the first time he had lied to avoid going to work. He wondered if people passing didn't see that his chest was open and a wound bleeding. When Helena Lund came she looked surprised and pleased to see him.

'Did you not think I would come?' he asked.

She touched his wet coat sleeve.

'You mustn't fall in love with me,' she said.

7

Raphael Newell outwalked the centre of the city and came to the railings of the Vigeland park. There was a plaque and the name of the sculptor Gustav Vigeland whose bronze figures filled the park. The lock on the pedestrian gate was faulty or had been forced, and Ray passed inside to take a closer look. Beneath his feet the frozen gravel made a noise of bones. Figures were floodlit in amber. Vigeland had installed in a myriad of forms, figures of every age, children, youths, middle-aged men and women, those in advanced old age, all caught in poses of different emotions. It was as if he had tried to imprison in bronze every aspect of human existence, from joy to grief, anger to jubilation, every phase of life. Each figure was entirely realistic, but weirdly still with a grave unutterable sorrow. To walk among them, man after woman, child after grandfather, was disconcerting. Deeper into the park, above an unmoving fountain, was the centrepiece of Vigeland's work, a high granite obelisk, known as 'the Monolit'. Here was a tower of humanity, a mad column of figures writhing, climbing, clambering over each other to reach the top, each one uniquely sculpted, each one with an individual face and expression as they attempted to get higher and higher up towards the sky. Against the dark of the sky there appeared a mass of children at the top. The moment Ray came upon them he wanted to look away. It was too strange. Who were these people? Who had modelled for these figures? How did the sculptor imagine them one on top of the other scrambling toward the heavens? It was an image deeply troubling to him; there was something about it he couldn't bear.

Ray had turned away and decided to go back to the hotel when he saw a man edging out from behind one of the statues further down the park. Had someone followed him in? Was there someone now waiting to attack him? He tightened his right fist on the closed lapels of his coat and lowered his chin. The man had slipped out of sight again. But of course it wasn't an attacker, Ray told himself. That's not what's going to happen, that's not why I came all this way. He talked himself into a thin faith but walked cautiously back down the gravel-way. Then he heard, just above the noise of his footsteps, words being spoken in German. Was there more than one man? Was it some kind of illicit encounter? Brusquely he beat his feet on the path hurrying past. The talking stopped at once. Out from the side of one of the bronzes there appeared an older man in a dark overcoat and woollen hat. He wore black-framed glasses. There appeared to be no one else with him, or perhaps whoever it was had ducked back around the other side. The man looked out at Ray with the flat expression of someone caught in inexplicable circumstance. He opened his mouth and raised a hand as though to pause any interpretation and commence a long defence. Ray had stopped. He wanted to tell the man he had made no judgement, and that whatever was happening was of no importance to him, that he was no threat. But even as he was thinking this, even in the briefest of interludes in which he was wondering if there was any word he knew in German or even if it was German he had heard, or if he said a German word would the man think he had been eavesdropping – even in that instant, Ray was realizing he recognized the stranger. He was – astonishingly – the bald man from the flight earlier. He was the man sitting mumbling in dream. Ray was sure of it. But as this knowledge arrived the man had dropped his hand and turned and was hurrying off across the pale frosted grass.

'Wait! Wait, stop, it's all right!'

The man did not turn back. He vanished beyond the amber floodlight into the dark.

8

'Can I ask you . . . ?'

'Yes.'

'The sadness you talk about . . . is it . . . ?'

They were sitting in the National Concert Hall. Earlier, in the museum, Helena had mentioned loving the music of Chopin and Raphael had remembered there was an evening concert of the Nocturnes performed by John O Connor and been emboldened to order tickets. Now, in the hum of the hall, watching the audience arrive and unwing from their damp Dublin overcoats, he felt such a surge of happiness, of hopefulness, that he imagined he could banish any sadness. He turned to Helena. He was still falling. The depth was extraordinary. He already knew he was calling in sick the following day and the one after and again until the moment she would leave, and beyond that he didn't think.

'What sadness?'

'You said yesterday . . .'

'This is my week. I am not talking of sadness. All sadness is gone. Only the beautiful sadness of Chopin.'

'But . . .'

'No.'

Applause like a flight of birds was released. John O Connor walked from the wings. He sat before the polished black piano, made two small adjustments of the stool, and then paused. There was an instant of complete stillness; his hands were open and above the keys, on his face a focus sublime, as if he was about to engage in the most extraordinary act of resurrection.

9

When Ray returned to the hotel he was frozen through. He climbed into the stiff embrace of the bed, but couldn't sleep. He rose and put on the hotel dressing gown and sat by the radiator at the window, watching the icy emptiness of Oslo. He was not impatient or even tired. Rather he felt he had already experienced the renewal of rest and was ready for the morning to come when he could find Helena Lund. He had her address. His intention was to take a taxi there and knock on her door. What consequence would flow from this he didn't allow himself to consider. Carefully he guarded within himself the lover's illusion that love is all that matters. It was not important that she was not expecting him. It was what he *had* to do.

Never before in his life had Ray felt quite like this. The youthful passion and devotion he had felt for Marjorie seemed to him of a lesser order. With Helena there was an extra element of zeal, of absolute commitment, a sense of mission, something apostolic even, in its Greek origin of being *sent*. Nor was this the only significant difference. As he sat with his feet in socks against the radiator, Ray was visited by feelings of intense beatitude. Not something he could have characterized as a feeling before, and certainly not as one belonging to his life, he thought at first it was to do with the difficult flight, then perhaps the astonishing clarity of the Norwegian air. Was he light-headed? Things struck him now, shapes, shadows, smells, music, all in some way clarified, illumined. It was as if a great clap of inspiration had resounded and everything beneath it quivered and was then just so much more clearly itself.

It was impossible to explain; the world seemed *gifted* to Raphael Newell and as he sat in the small hours he received it with gladness. Time slipped away and no tiredness came; if anything the inspiration became more charged and the vision brighter. As if dreaming, he thought of the world as a great flat surface and he with the perspective of an eagle flying. He could see day and night, the division of light, those awake or asleep, the moving and the still, the numberless multitudes that yet were numbered. Out across the city rooftops he suddenly imagined the world, and from this imagining caught something of all that was common to human existence, the loving and hatred, the ambition and hope and endeavour, passion, prejudice, ever-expanding lexicon of desire, the planet entire throbbing with infinitesimal yearning.

It was unlike him. He was an accountant from Dublin. He was neither religious nor visionary, but in that waking night sat by the window in the Hotel Chester and would not have been surprised if anyone who had seen him from the street said that he was on fire.

10

'Newell, are you dying? This is your fourth day. I mentioned it to Mr Whitton and he agreed it was most unlike you, you were never sick. So I suppose it's pretty bad whatever it is. And we're sorry of course. But well, things are piling up here – you know business of life doesn't stop – and well, I said I'd call and enquire. So, I hope you get this message and well, maybe we'll see you tomorrow. Oh, this is Bradley, by the way.'

11

In his room arranged fanlike on the side table were three books. Ray took one of them with him to breakfast at seven o'clock. It was still dark outside but the city was moving to work. He sat in the low light of the breakfast-room where two other guests were breakfasting behind newspapers. He smiled at his waiter, ordered coffee and eggs with ham. The book was a general guide to Oslo, and Ray thought it proper to know something of the city – 'The name derives from an old Norse word for God, *As*, and *Lo* meaning field.' While he waited, he read of the Vigeland park and saw photographs of the sculptures that made them look ordinary. There was a section on the Church of Saint Olav, and another on the paintings of Edvard Munch. These, with titles like *Despair* and *Anxiety*, were not in keeping with Ray's optimism. Then of course there was the celebrated *The Scream*. In the guidebook it said that Munch had painted over fifty versions of this. There was a quote from him about how he came to paint it.

'*I was walking along a road with two friends. The sun set. I felt a tinge of melancholy. Suddenly the sky became blood red. I stopped and leaned against a railing feeling exhausted, and I looked at the flaming clouds that hung like blood and a sword over the blue-black fjord and the city. My friends walked on. I stood there trembling with fright. And I felt an unending scream piercing nature.'*

The moment he read this, Ray felt a chill at the back of his neck, and closed the book, as if he had intruded somewhere. As he did he noticed one of the other guests just then leaving was the raven-haired woman from the plane. How extraordinary!

After breakfast he got his coat and in the lobby was greeted warmly by the manager Avner.

'Cold outside today, Mr Newell.'

'Yes. I'm sure.'

'Very cold. But not for you, you go walking?'

It was too early to go to the apartment address.

'For a while, yes.'

'You like our city.' It seemed a statement of fact; Avner smiled behind it.

Ray returned a weak smile and headed outside. The cold was intense and startling, the pasty light of the sky like a smeared ointment. Upon the paths wan-faced figures buttoned to their chins hastened as though on urgent errands. He walked down Karl Johan's Gate, took a side street, and wandered between shadow and light, feeling build in him the anticipation of seeing Helena. At one point the idea of him being there, he, Raphael Newell, flying to a foreign city for the love of a woman who did not and could not love him, was so incongruous, so wildly removed from who he had been, that he laughed out loud. Wasn't it marvellous? Wasn't it so extraordinary that everything else in his life to this point seemed pale and insubstantial? His feelings amplified. He thought of her face. He thought of small details in her skin that he had not known he had noticed. There was a mole low down on her neck. There were three wrinkles, sister rivers, running from the corner of both of her eyes. They deepened when she smiled, and when she smiled there was knowledge and sadness. A scar on her wrist, the fair hair on her lower forearm as her sleeve withdrew, the purse of her lips when thinking.

Through such images in lover's delight, Ray was walking when he noticed one of the large department stores had opened, and out of the cold he went inside. Should he buy her something? Shouldn't he bring something? He had in his mind the idea of perfume. Normally he would have considered this too intimate a gift, and been fearful of her husband's objection, but in the state he was in all such cautions vanished; it didn't matter. He was acting out of pure feeling, and supposed this to be a blessed state in which there could be no wrong. If he could find her scent, he thought. If he only knew which one it was. He moved in warm brightness past Special Offers and soon noticed that in Perfume just in front of him there was some commotion. A man, short, dark-haired Japanese, appeared to be opening the boxes of different bottles of scent and misting them in the air. Beside him was a shop assistant explaining in Norwegian that he must stop. On the floor at his feet were several empty cartons and even as the saleswoman was growing more agitated and shaking both of her hands in a waving gesture across her chest, the man was taking another brand and spraying it. It was then that Ray recognized him.

'Wait, wait a minute, stop.' An unlikely peacemaker, Ray came forward into the tangled cloud of *Opium*, *Passion* and *Oblivion*.

The man turned, a pitiful expression on his face. There was a deep furrow across his glistening brow, a trapped desperation in his eyes. Ray held up his hand like a London policeman.

'You must stop,' he said calmly. By now there was gathered a small gallery. 'You must buy the perfume or leave it back,' Ray idiotically explained to the man, as though he were newly landed on earth and not yet used to its customs.

The saleswoman who was tall was a kind of polished metallic figure with hair dyed titanium. Her eyes were frantic green. She didn't want this mess in her section. She wanted her days to match the beige neutrality of the piped musak.

'It's all right, just a misunderstanding I'm sure,' Raphael Newell reassured her, and stooped and picked up a number of the torn cartons.

'Now,' he said to the man, in a tone for the insane or small children, 'we'll put these back, all right? For some there are "testers", you see,' he pointed to one. 'But mostly you have to just go by the packaging.' There was a bottle in the shape of a headless woman's body, and this the man now sprayed as though he had understood nothing.

'No, stop. Really.' Ray was dismayed, his peacekeeping failing. The metallic saleswoman had a frown forged deeply into her brow.

'I must find it!' said the man.

'You speak English?'

'I find it! I find it. Here.' He flipped open his wallet and produced a credit card that he pressed into Ray's hand. 'I will buy them.'

'Yes, that's fine, whichever, that's . . .' Ray was trying to extricate himself.

'All.'

'Sorry?'

'All. I will buy all.'

Ray looked at the Japanese man, he seemed exactly the kind of businessman found in a thousand cities of the world, only there was moisture silvered in the lines of his forehead, and the bright gloss of his eyes made him seem a little mad.

'Why? Why would you buy them all?'

But already the man was moving along the rows of women's scents, taking one of each. In the florid air Ray stood watching. The saleswoman, having seen the credit card, had returned to her cash desk. In a moment Ray calculated that the Japanese man had a thousand euro worth of perfumes dropped on the counter, and in another few moments had gone and brought back the same quantity again. He moved with fixed focus. Nothing distracted him, not Raphael Newell's standing nearby, nor the mess of opened cartons on the floor, nor the little gathering slowly dispersing. He took one of everything, as though he was engaged in deep and exhaustive research and could not allow the possibility of a single oversight.

It was a weird scene, and Ray felt compelled to attend it. He was *attached* to it. He conjectured reasons for the odd behaviour. Perhaps the man was impossibly wealthy, perhaps he was seeking a scent he had inhaled at a party and wanted to bring back to Japan to his wife. Or his mistress in Tokyo had requested one particular perfume from Europe, one he had brought back to her before. But now he had forgotten its name and was forced to chase it on the air eyes shut, imagining as he did that he lay on a tatami and breathed it on his lover's thigh.

Such things Ray thought as the man hurried up and down, adding more and more perfumes. He thought of Helena Lund and the scent she wore that was like almonds and rain. He read the name on the American Express card, Tanaka, Tekeshi.

'Mr Tanaka,' he said, 'perhaps you have enough.'

'I think I have all.'

'Yes, I think you have.'

He made a slight bow as he took back his credit card, then offered it for payment.

The tall saleswoman had already sub-totalled nearly twenty-four thousand kroner. She looked at the credit card sceptically then slid it through the machine and waited. She hadn't yet started bagging the various bottles of perfume. It occurred to Ray that the entire episode was a set-up, and that at any moment someone might step out with a camera and announce it had all been part of a televised prank. He prepared to smile graciously and nod. He was prepared to have Mr Tanaka turn and grin and slap him on the back. But the little buzz-printing of the credit-card bill seemed real, and Mr Tanaka did lean down and sign it. He looked down the aisle for telltale signs of this being a production, of being caught in some Norwegian TV show: *The Man Who Bought All the Perfume in the World.*

But nothing happened. Mr Tanaka waited while the woman bagged the perfumes. Then he picked them up and hurried away. There was not the slightest indication that he was mad or that he had spent over three thousand euro just to track down a perfume. Ray couldn't help himself, he followed out after him and walked some yards behind, unsure whether to say anything or not. At last, on the opposite side of the street, the man found an old building with steps up to imposing locked doors. There, in his black suit and overcoat, he sat and began opening the perfumes. He misted a spray on the cold air and sniffed at it. He discarded each bottle on the ground and tore open another. From across the road Raphael Newell watched. The scene had a strange hold on him; the man's bizarre quest, tearing open the boxes, spraying some scents and dabbing others on his wrist, the back of his hand, and in time further up his arm, was reminiscent of Arabic fairy tale or legend. Was there something about magic and a woman being trapped inside a bottle for years and years, waiting an improbable time until her lover would at last find and release her? Ray wished he could remember.

Systematically Mr Tanaka opened bottle after bottle of perfume. He was soon a little island to himself, and sat in the all but visible cloud of a thousand flowers that hung about him. Ray looked in a bookshop window at titles in Norwegian. Then he glanced back. Still the man was spraying the scents. Ray went away a little so as not to be staring, pretended interest in a display of vacuum cleaners. Then he returned his gaze to the scene on the steps. Mr Tanaka had almost come to the end of the perfumes he had bought. They lay scattered, a brightly coloured litter about his feet. He misted the last one and sniffed at it, and then he let out a cry. It was a noise loud enough to travel the distance down the street where Ray was standing at the shop window. It was a cry of exultation; at last Mr Tanaka had found what he was looking for, and his entire body now convulsed in joy. He held the bottle in his trembling hand and looked at it. He sprayed the perfume again and shut his eyes to breathe it in. Then to the heavens he made a loud long cheer.

Ray looked away; strangely he felt the scene was almost unbearable. There was something naked there, and suddenly he had to get away. He couldn't watch any more.

Raphael Newell pressed his hands deep into his coat pockets; he lowered his head and hurried away.

12

They walked along the Grand Canal. She wore a coat of soft green tweed. She told him about her children, how they were musical and bright, the delight she took in them. She worked in community arts. Her husband was an engineering consultant for an oil company. Ray listened.

On the narrow towpath he walked alongside, in his shone black shoes side-stepping puddles. In moments when he brushed against her he felt the touch of something sublime, as if onto his fingers gold leaf flaked from a masterpiece.

They stopped in cafes for the rain to pass.

'You can take these days from work?' she asked him.

'O yes. They think I'm dying,' he said.

'You have a lovely smile. See, like that, yes. A shy smile.'

'You are very kind.'

'No, not really.'

'I think I am in love with you.'

'Shsh. Don't say that.'

'No, it's true. I know I am. And it's all right. There's nothing you have to do. I am not expecting anything. I don't want anything really. Just I had to tell you.'

Helena Lund reached across and put her hand on top of where his two hands held together like a knot. She left her touch there a moment then withdrew it. 'You are such a kind man,' she said.

'No, I'm not,' Ray said, his face bright, his eyes polished with daring. He spoke quickly. 'There is something that happened when I saw you, and really I knew straight away, and you see, I knew there was no hope, and normally that would be enough to stop me, to stop anything happening. But this wasn't like that. This was like something that existed already, you see? It was like it wasn't up to me; I am just to love you, that's all. And to keep on doing it no matter what, because that's, that's what this is. It's the nature of it. And what I want to believe is that it will be of some use to you.'

'Use?'

'Yes. This love. That it's not just something for me, my own, I don't know, entertainment. Something to fill up my days. But that it's real, and that it comes from a source like a spring down underneath everything and that it's true and good somehow, you know, flowing up out of the goodness in the world itself, this love.'

Helena turned to the cafe window streaked with rain. 'Maybe you are a saint,' she said.

13

From Oslo city centre Ray went by taxi to the southern suburbs. He had her address, though he couldn't quite remember when he got it. He sat in the back seat and tried to move the scene of Mr Tanaka from his mind. He watched the grave buildings of the city retreat and the thickening loops of rail and road bearing commuters. Above him the morning sky was the heavy grey from which he had descended the day before. There was little light. But the gloom affected him not at all. In fact, he was fired by the emotion he carried and experienced that most rare of things, the sense of being in perfect synchronization with the secret engine of the world. It was, it suddenly occurred to him, the most natural thing: how love surfaced in each of us, unexpected, unbidden even, but undeniable. That it had happened in even such a small life as his made it all the more remarkable. Across the positive and negative terminals of his mind such insights fizzed and flashed. He longed to see her face again. He longed to be sitting just across from her and to listen to her talking, simply to be in her presence. He wanted to watch her hands moving as she spoke, the way she talked. Raphael Newell did not think if this was right or wrong, if it was incorrect or objectification or sexist, or what she might say when she saw him on her doorstep. He had an absolute faith that from love comes goodness, and sat in the taxi no different to a gleaming knight riding to the horizon.

The suburbs were stacked; mid-sized apartment buildings shouldered around small green spaces frozen off-white. He paid the taxi driver, and as the car drove away, leaving him alone, Ray felt the thrill of arrival. It was half-past nine. Between the buildings there was an air of serene emptiness, employees and schoolchildren departed. The path was a salted passageway between icy edges. He looked around for Apartment Block 12–20 and, finding it, walked with the careful gait of those suspicious of the treachery of ice. Still, how wonderful it was! How simply bizarre, that he was there, that he had made it! The cold air pulled tight his skin, made clear his nostrils. He had the sense of his whole person being tightened, firmed by the freezing conditions. His eyes widened, his short hair stood. There was an intensely pure quality in those moments. It was as if he had arrived in another element, not quite the world as it had been before. This was not the dog-eared comfortable complacent place that had been his experience. This was an absolute, a kind of clear clean distillation in which to those newly arrived on the planet the very air would seem of miraculous immaculateness. Ray took parcels of breath and watched the plume of himself expire. He had again the feeling that he was going to laugh out loud. It rose up through him and watered in his eyes.

The building she lived in was dull and functional and without personality. The lift was an aluminium box. He pressed 5, and watched the two halves of himself meet in his reflection as the doors closed.

When he arrived before her apartment, Raphael Newell's heartbeat was a drum loud enough for him not to need the doorbell. But he rang it anyway, then took a half step back so that he would not frighten her.

14

Ray wanted to kiss her, but knew he couldn't. When she got up from his side and crossed the bar of Dublin's Abbey Theatre at the intermission, he shuddered with desire. Anyone who might have glanced in his direction would have seen the white blossoms bursting from his fingers.

15

He waited a good time. There was no answer. In case she had a tap running or was on the phone, he rang the doorbell again. Perhaps she had taken the children to school, he thought. He returned to the lift and stepped in beside an elderly woman who looked at him suspiciously. Ray passed her a small smile. 'I'm just visiting,' he said. But either the woman did not understand or saw through the thinness of this lie. She tightened her mouth and made a low sound of disapproval. Ray didn't care. Nothing it seemed could unsettle or disturb the solid floor of faith inside him. He was a zealot for this love. The usual considerations and doubts that in his cautious earlier life would have cracked through in a thousand places – that he would be a burden to her, an embarrassment, a bother, that he shouldn't have come, would cause her upset, rows with her husband – mattered to Raphael Newell not at all. It simply wouldn't be like that, he believed. He wanted nothing, only to be near. With the pale naivety of the absolute innocent, he saw nothing but happiness ahead. He had savings in the bank. He had a talent for accountancy and could eventually work there. It was as if he had reached his right arm toward the table in his mind where lay stacked the jumble of objections, and with a single movement he had swept them all away. It was unlike him; but that was a cornerstone of this loving. Helena Lund had changed him completely, so he was this other, better, version of himself.

He came outside again into the cold. The old woman eyed him as if he were a thief.

'Hva gjor De her?' she asked.

Ray did not understand. 'I love her,' he said.

But perhaps the old woman thought it was her he meant and that this declaration was a cruel mockery; it pierced where she had lost her love a wartime ago. Loudly she replied in Norwegian. Her eyebrows lowered intently, she flung at him three, four sentences, long and animated and incomprehensible. Perhaps she was explaining to him things he couldn't know yet. Perhaps she was telling him the nature of love in time, or how she herself knew what for him was ahead. In the urgent instants of her admonishment she was like those statues that guard doorways, and come to life upon the approach of villain or hero.

'I'm sorry,' Ray said, holding up his hands.

The woman shook her head. Tightly she held to her grey bag.

'Her,' he pointed back at the building. 'Helena. I love *Helena*.'

The name, said out loud, stopped her. Her small brown eyes narrowed, and she reached her hand onto his arm. She spoke again in Norwegian, but this time more softly, as if pressing upon him secrets. Ray understood not a single word. He smiled politely; he nodded. But the woman wanted him to understand and repeated what she had said. Then she did the most extraordinary thing. She leaned forward and kissed the side of Ray's face. It was a cold soft touch, an instant, no more, and as she withdrew the expression in her face was of sorrow and pity. She said no more, and before Ray could think of how to respond, she had turned and walked off down the icy path. As she did – her back was to him, so he couldn't be sure, and Norwegians are not religious – Ray thought he saw her bless herself.

He felt he should say something. He should call after her. But he didn't.

Beneath the pressure of the infinite blue above, the grey sky had begun to flake. Soon all the air was blind with snow.

16

'Newell, really, we are quite worried. Are you all right? I'm wondering if I should come around. Do you need anything? Well, do call and let us know. It's just that it's so unlike you. I suppose everybody gets ill, but. Well, things still piling up of course. Oh, Mr Whitton says hello and get well and the usual. So – I hate talking to these things, like talking to a bloody ghost – anyway if you need anything, as I said, just give a tinkle and I'll drop round. Right? Right, then. Goodbye.'

Helena was standing listening to the machine

when Ray returned from the kitchen with a bottle of red wine and two glasses.

'They think you are ill?' she said.

'Yes.'

'That's hilarious.'

He uncorked the bottle and poured. 'I had to give an excuse. I didn't think I could tell the truth.'

'You could. You could say you were entertaining a friend.'

'I'd want to say I have fallen in love.'

'No.'

'It's the truth.' His hand trembled passing her the glass.

'You can't be in love with me. You don't know me. But maybe you are in love with the idea that you could love again, and that is a delicious thing. Very intoxicating.'

He thought for a second about this. 'Oh no,' he said, quite simply. 'It's you.'

They drank the wine. The house was quiet;

she asked him if he had music. He had bought the Nocturnes of Chopin, and put this on the player. He sat across from her.

'I'd do anything for you,' he said.

She smiled, touched, and moved a fall of hair back from her face. Her legs were curved beneath her on the couch. Lamplight made golden her skin, and bestowed an impossible beauty. 'I don't want you to do anything. In two days I will be gone.'

Ray pressed his hands together. He felt the contrary emptiness and fullness of those who have given all of themselves, and still feel this is not enough. The impulse to do more, to express, to release what inside him kept filling even as he emptied it, was overpowering. He wanted to buy her presents; that morning he had met her with two bouquets of purple tulips and she had carried them about with her. But even these, as they sat bowing now in a vase on the table, seemed inadequate. There should be more flowers, and more beautiful ones. In fevered vision, he saw a version of himself briefly become an omnipotent creator, hurrying just ahead of her down the street, transforming whatever was plain or dull, making blue the sky, and rose petals of the path. He was burdened with enormous longing, and no matter what he did, Raphael Newell could not feel it was enough. Was there no end to it? Would the impossibility of her loving him not close his heart, hurt him into quiet?

The problem was Ray could not believe such love as he felt was wrong. He knew there would be no affair. He knew Helena Lund existed in some other world beyond him. But with the clear dispassion of an accountant, he knew too that the emotion flowing into him was totalling in Credit, and to her must be of value.

'It has to be for the good,' he said, when he had walked her back to her hotel and she had left her kiss on the top of his head. 'It has to be for something, this love.'

When he arrived home the Nocturnes were still playing on Repeat. There was no possibility of sleep. He sat in the armchair and looked at the couch where she had been.

17

Through the snow he walked from the apartment buildings down to the road where he imagined he might see her returning. The snowflakes were thick and heavier than any he had known. They all but filled the air. He faced up into them, the off-white unpacking of the sky, his hair and shoulders briefly starred. In this, as in all things now, he found rapture. The exquisite beauty of the snow fall, the individual trajectory of each flake, those that melted on contact and others that didn't, the silence that seemed to accompany the fall, such things. Alone in the scene, Ray thought it beyond the power of words. The loveliness of that ordinary place of road and building appeared to him to be infinite. He shuddered with flashes of insight: how angles of rooflines met or made patterns mathematical and exact, how thin drifts of snow veiled a dozen windscreens, how everything seemed *designed*. Unlike himself, beneath the force of rapture; he wanted to hold out his arms to the heavens. He wanted to stand cruciform and hello the world like some human halleluia.

The snow fell. Few cars came, like dream versions of themselves, slow and purring. With each one Ray expected it might be Helena. But it wasn't. Cold came up from his feet. He stamped a dark imprint, crunched across to another viewpoint. At last a man arrived. He wore a thick duffel coat with hood and carried a brown-paper bag of groceries. He nodded at

Ray and passed by, then stopped. He asked something in Norwegian.

'I'm sorry, I don't understand.'

'Are you all right? This is not where the bus stops.'

'Oh no. Thank you very much. I'm waiting for somebody to come.'

'I see.' The man turned away.

'Her name is Helena. She lives just . . .'

The man had swung about. 'Helena Lund?' he asked.

'Yes. You know her?'

'I am Petter. I am her husband.' The man faced Ray. He was thick-shouldered and dark haired, in his grey eyes concern.

'I am Raphael Newell, Ray.' He held out his hand. 'From Dublin.'

'What is this about?'

Ray's hand hung there. The snow was falling. He felt a sudden panic at his heart, and knew he had to hide the truth.

'She won a prize,' he said. 'In Dublin, she entered this lottery. And she won. And I am here to . . . em . . . to give it to her. The prize.' He was a hopeless liar. If he was not so cold his face would have been scarlet.

'I see. You can give it to me, then.'

'Oh no. I'm very sorry. I have to hand it over personally. Company rules.'

Petter Lund looked at the small timid-looking man in the snow-shouldered overcoat and wet shoes. He must have weighed the threat and found it insubstantial. He said, 'She is at a meeting in the city, in the Arts Institute. She will be there until midday. You can come back then.'

'Yes, that's wonderful. I will. Thank you very much.' Ray turned and hurried away, his shoes slipping, so to Petter Lund watching he seemed a strange figure barely affixed to the turning world.

Ray caught the bus back into Oslo. He got

off at Karl Johan's Gate and asked for directions to the Arts Institute. The snow thickening, he arrived there at eleven twenty and stood across the street by a phone box to wait for her.

18

On her final night, Helena stayed with him in his house in Rathmines. She lay back against his chest while the Chopin played. He rested his hand on the white cashmere sleeve and breathed the scent of her hair. He did not try to kiss her, nor to do anything which might make her leave. She was the white dove that had landed in his heart.

'Do you ever think of dying?' she said. 'I do. I think of some terrible accident out there waiting for me. Love is an accident, so too is death. Everything is chance.'

Ray did not agree with her, but didn't say so.

In accountancy there is no chance, all proceeds with mathematical certainty towards the absolute truth. The light was low, night turning into day.

'You will miss me,' she said.

'Yes.'

'Don't be sad.'

Ray didn't answer. He didn't yet know how he would live the next day. If he thought of her going, he felt ill.

She lay with her back against him in her jeans and white cashmere sweater. For a brief time she slept.

Though he prayed it wouldn't, though he asked for time itself to pause and for the peace he knew then to continue, morning moved toward the window and light entered. Helena stirred. She looked back at Ray and blinked as if remembering how she had come there. 'Definitely a saint,' she said and smiled and kissed the top of his head as she stood.

He drove her to her hotel and then to the airport. He tried to put on a brave face, but he felt the dove being ripped from his chest and its claws clinging and from the vessels of his heart blood spouting everywhere.

When he returned home, he sat on the couch in the same position where she had lain against him.

He did not move from there.

19

It was eleven thirty. He checked his watch every few minutes. Carefully Ray kept his eye on the door. In large flakes the snow was still falling.

'You, it is you.' It was the bearded German hiker from the plane. He had been coming along the path when he noticed Ray standing there. 'I am Georg, you remember?'

'Yes. Yes I do.'

'Wonderful, eh?'

'I'm sorry?'

'Wonderful, this.'

Ray wasn't sure to what he was referring – the city, the snow – and in truth he didn't really care. He didn't want to be distracted; a moment and he would miss her.

But in the expression of the German there was something arresting. And in a moment Ray knew it was knowledge. Georg *knew* something, and whatever it was, yet unclear, but approaching rapidly now, turned Ray's stomach.

'This,' Georg said again. Then to demonstrate he closed his eyes and stepped backwards out into the traffic. Ray didn't have time to stop him, but watched with helpless compulsion as the blind Georg backed across two lines of cars and emerged untouched on the far side of the street. He stepped up on the path. 'I find Olga now,' he shouted, and gave a broad laugh and then continued away.

The knowledge was close now. A cool sweat was on Ray's brow, and he thought he might fall down. Snow was swirling wildly out of the heavens, as if each flake was a fragment of a message unread. Not taking his eyes from the doorway of the Institute, he stepped into the phone box and dialled Dublin.

Bradley answered.

'Bradley, it's me, Newell.'

The phone hung up. He called again.

'Bradley, don't hang up. I just need you to tell me everything is all right.'

'Whoever you are, this is a cruel joke.'

And again he hung up the phone.

Across the snow-street there was still no sign of her. But now Raphael Newell *knew*. He knew that in an instant she would appear, and, even as he opened the door of the phone box, he was filled with such enlightenment and love he would not have been surprised to learn his radiance made him seem halo-ed.

And there, at last, Helena Lund was coming. She was hurrying because she was late and had to collect one of her children. She wore a black coat and a white scarf and blinked at the heaviness of the snow swirling and stepped out between two parked cars.

She did not see the bus coming.

But Ray did. He saw everything at the same time. He saw himself in Dublin on the days after she had left him. He saw how he had been unable to move, how he had locked the door and disconnected the phone, and lay on the couch slowly burning with love until he was only ashes in the corner of the room. He saw Bradley finding him there two weeks later, and the small funeral in the rain. All such passed through Raphael Newell in a single instant, and he knew he had returned for a single purpose and he called out a warning to Helena Lund across the snow-street.

Her surprise at seeing him stopped her sharply.

The bus that was to have killed her passed by.

Helena looked across the street, but already he was gone. In white ecstasy he was ascending.

Invisible, swift, clothed in rapture, Raphael Newell passed up and up again, through the falling snow and on above the tallest buildings of that city, back through the thick hem of grey that held the world. He climbed like a white dove, purposeful and triumphant, climbing and continuing on and on through the grey and the more grey, until he came out at last into the eternal cathedral of blissful blue.

PICADOR SHOTS

SHALOM AUSLANDER
'Holocaust Tips for Kids' and 'Smite the Heathens, Charlie Brown' from *Beware of God*

CRAIG DAVIDSON
'A Mean Utility' and 'Life in the Flesh' from *Rust and Bone*

BRET EASTON ELLIS
'Water from the Sun' and 'Discovering Japan' from *The Informers*

NELL FREUDENBERGER
'Lucky Girls' from *Lucky Girls*

ALEKSANDAR HEMON
'Exchange of Pleasant Words' and 'A Coin' from *The Question of Bruno*

JACKIE KAY
'Sonata' from *Wish I Was Here*

MATTHEW KNEALE
'Powder' from *Small Crimes in An Age of Abundance*

CLAIRE MESSUD
'The Professor's History'

JAMES SALTER
'My Lord You' and 'Palm Court' from *Last Night*

COLM TÓIBÍN
'The Use of Reason' from *Mothers and Sons*

NIALL WILLIAMS
unpublished new story – 'The Unrequited'

TIM WINTON
'Small Mercies' from *The Turning*

All collections are available in Picador.